Bibliographic information of the German National Library. The Deutsche Nationalbibliothek lists this publication in the German National Bibliography. Detailed bibliographic information is available on the Internet at http://dnb.dnb.de.

© 2020 Karl-Heinz Rüster

Production and publishing

BoD - Books on Demand, Norderstedt

ISBN: 9 783751 967143

Death in the Everglades

It became known early this morning, the three people who had been missing for four days have been found deep in the Everglades. According to news reports, the three were found dead. There bodies have since been taken to the morgue. The media continues to report that the three had suffered a horrible death. According to friends, the three were on an Airboat ride from Everglades City towards Everglades National Park for an "exploration", they were accompanied by an experienced Miccosukee Indian. Because they had not returned late in the evening, a major search operation was initiated by the Miccosukee Police department.

The identities of the dead were swiftly determined as two of the dead carried ID cards. The Captain of the airboat was identified as Will (Eagle) Osceola, he was personally known to the investigators. The other two were Chris Apples and Stan McPride.

The FBI was asked for assistance by the Seminole/Miccosukee Police Department because one of the dead was not an American citizen. Stan McPride was English.

My name is Phil Millner, a detective at the FBI Field Department in Fort Myers, and I was assigned to investigate with my longtime colleague Bert Hunt. We immediately started the investigation. Bert and I went to the scene of the accident, where the three were found. The site could only be reached by airboat or helicopter.

It is located about 11 miles southeast of Everglades City.

The Scenic Loop Road Drive, the closest way to meet people, is 9 miles east. To the North, US 41 (Tamiami Trail) is over 8 miles away. The site is in a sense in the midst of the Everglades.

The scene was extremely grisly even to an experienced police officer who has seen and experienced quite a bit. The airboat was about a mile from the spot where the three men had been found. It was overturned in the shallow water. It was very difficult, even from a helicopter, to identify. Two of the bodies were close together, the other about 800 yards away, closer to the overturned airboat.

Two of the dead had to be cut from the swamp, because they had become entangled in creepers and laid in the knee-deep water. Only the heads of the dead still stood out of the clear water, disfigured by mosquitoes and other creatures, beyond recognition. The dead man, who was found closer to the airboat was not as disfigured as the other two but also was littered by innumerable insect bites.

The forensic team noticed a large laceration at the back of his head, and two punctures or bite marks on his left arm, that were very hard to detect. His legs and arms were bitten by insects too, but recognizable. He was later identivied as Will (Eagle) Osceola.

The scenario itself was a bit unreal, the poor visibility and the shimmering heat, and the light mist over the swamp, did the rest. I've never seen anything like it before, they had no chance to escape the swamp. They must have suffered a terrible death.

We both left and talked on the way back to Fort Myers to the Field Department, about what we had just experienced and seen.

"Was it an accident?" I said to Bert, there was no evidence of a foreign influence to be seen.The laceration at the head of the Indian guide may have come from the accident of the airboat. The other two had probably got tangled in the plants and could not free themselves. Had they tried to rearrange the overturned airboat and had exhausted themselves in the attempt, and then were too weak to free themselves from the plants? If they had tried to walk the way back, a difficult task in itself, only the Indian probably had the necessary experience to create a path.

The swamp is a challenge to anyone trying. And I've noticed that the two of them had gone the wrong way out, this would have taken them even deeper into the Everglades because they were heading south instead of west towards Everglades City or east to Scenic Loop Drive.

Will Osceola, the Miccosukee Airboat captain, the one had been found closer to the overturned boat, probably had a snake encounter and that cost him his life, presumably! The punctures on his left arm make it likely.

These are all questions that need to be clarified. I'm curious to see what results the forensics department comes up with. For example, what is the exact cause of death? I'll have to apply for an autopsy on the men when I'm back in the office. I didn't have any phone signal out here.

As far as I can judge, there is no apparent reason to suspect foul play in the death of the three men. I think it was a terrible accident. Bert agreed, he too could not see any third-party involvement at this time.

Arriving at the office, we wrote the inevitable report and thought the case was done. The rest is routine and is handled by the individual departments. So our mission was over, we thought.

A few days later, I had a report from the forensics department on my desk. The case was already puzzling me and I began to doubt the cause of death. Was it not an accident, as we first suspected?

The report said: "The Miccosukee Indian died from a high dose of snake venom, but the bite marks on his left arm are actually too small for that. It is thought that they look more like pinpricks ".

How the other two dead people could get tangled up in creepers, even for the forensic specialist, is a mystery. The exact causes of death are still under investigation.

The creepers in the wetlands are not sturdy enough to hold down an adult human. They are to tear with little effort, even a child would be able to pull free. I tried to imagine why the two could not free themselves from the plants. I came to no conclussion. I thought this all is very strange.

I tried to imagine the scenario:

"Kill three people, wrap two of the dead with the creepers, and tie the legs of the dead"? Then inject the third with snake venom," absurd, I rejected the thought. But why couldn't they free themselves from the plants? Is there still another possible scenario? At the moment I can't think of anybody or anything else. "I immediately called Bert to let him know the result.

Bert also had doubts, maybe there is another clue, he said. All of these questions needed to be answered urgently.

Where did the killer come from, if it was murder? The airboat had, according to witnesses, only the three people on board when it left the dock.

The autopsy report of the dead confirmed the first investigations of the forensic staff. The Miccosukee Indian succumbed to a high dose of snake venom found in his body (it was identified as the poison of a Cottonmouth Water Moccasin). But the bite marks on his arm are too tiny for them to come from a snake.

The other two probably died of weakness and the consequences of high temperatures. There were daytime temperatures of over 91 F with a very high humidity for the time of the day. And as always, the mosquitoes appear in myriad swarms.

The Seminole Police Department informed me a day later that the two dead, except the airboat captain, belonged to a consortium based in Miami. According to Seminole colleagues, the consortium plans to build a huge city in the Everglades of Las Vegas style. It was called the Consortium for Development in Southwest Florida called, "CDSF" for short.

Hello, I thought, now things are getting very interesting. Bert said to me, "Have you ever heard anything about this? Plans to build a city in the middle of the Everglades?"

Upon further investigation, we came across links from the Consortium, to the Miccosukee and Seminole Tribes.

"We should visit the Seminole and Miccosukee Tribes, to see how much the clans knew about the disappearance and death of the three men, or about the plan of a city in the Everglades," I said.

The Seminole Indian Tribe owns a casino in Immokalee. The Miccosukee Tribe maintains a resort and casino in Miami. The tribe also runs gaming casinos on all of its lands. Miccosukee Casino is located on US 41, Tamiami Trail and Krome Avenue. All the casinos were very successful.

Bert said, "We should ask a colleague from the Seminole Police Department for assistance because the 'accident site' falls under their jurisdiction anyway."

I called the Seminole Police Department and we were assigned to colleague Harry (Snake) Cypres.

We contated Harry (Snake) Cypres the next morning and arranged to meet at the Miccosukee Resort and Gaming Casino in Miami.

Snake, as he preferred to be called, was a Special Deputy Officer of the Miccosukee Police Department. All deputies were responsible for crimes committed in the Indian Reservation.

Although there was no concrete suspicion of a crime yet, there should be no possibility left out. I was particularly interested in the connections of the tribes to the Consortium for Development in Southwest Florida, as they called themselves.

Initial investigations revealed that the consortium included some very influential people. Yes, even connections to higher circles in Washington could not be ruled out.

The consortium was based in Miami, at the most expensive location. There were no names yet, but one thing is clear so far, it's a very influential company with a huge financial background. There are some details that there also could be links to the Drug Mafia.

My colleagues from the relevant departments are already working feverishly on that matter.

It is getting more interesting!

We met in the evening at Miccosukee Gaming Resort and wanted to speak a few words with the chairman of the Miccosukee Council, but the secretary behind the front desk arrogantly denied us a meeting, claiming that no one from senior management was present.

Now I thought this is enough! I slammed my FBI badge on the desk and demanded to speak immediately to someone who is responsible for the operation of the resort.

That helped, she hustled back through the huge glass door and two minutes later she came back with a gentleman in her wake. He introduced himself as Rob (Deer) Peterson, the Assistant Chairman.

"How can I help you?" he asked, apologizing that his secretary had not informed him immediately. "Forget it," Snake said: *"Let's get to the point!"*

First, what is known by the tribe to build a city on the reservation ground?

Second, what kind of relationship did the three dead men from the Everglades have with the Miccosukee Tribe.

Third, did the tribe have any ties with the Consortium of Development in Southwest Florida?

Rob, Mr. Peterson, politely offered us a seat, and he also began to confirm that a few months ago a meeting with some members of the CDSF had taken place. But he was not aware of any details, as he was not present at the meeting personally. He knew, however, that the meeting was about planning a city on the reservation.

He also knew that there were quite a few supporters within the clans, but most of them strongly opposed such a development plan.

He regretted the tragic death of Will (Eagle) Osceola the Miccosukee Scout, who the others were, he did not know. "Where do the Seminoles and Miccosukee stand on this issue?" Snake asked. "There, too, I think, there are pros and cons," replied Mr. Peterson. "I tell you, it was discussed very hotly.

On one hand, this would mean a huge financial boost for our reservation, but on the other hand the majority of the Indian tribes fear the total destruction of the Everglades and thus of our habitat," he continued. "We owe so much to the River of Grass, "Kahayatle" as we call it. It saved our lives when we had to flee to the Everglades after the Seminole war. The Everglades have offered us protection from persecution. We as Seminoles and Miccosukee owe our existence to the Everglades. We will never forget that we have a spiritual contact with the Everglades, so to speak, it is a symbiosis. Both benefit from each other."

Snake commented to Bert and me, "He is right, the tribes are closely linked to the biosphere of the Everglades. There are only about 4,400 Seminole Tribe members in six Indian Reservations in Florida. There are also a few tribe members who refused to join the merger of the Miccosukee tribes of Florida in the 1962 separate recognition act of the US Government. Since then, they have been considered 'independent' Seminole. They are not officially recognized by the Federal Office of Indian Affairs. This group continues to protest against any government intervention in their lives. They also maintain an open land claim with the federal government for much of the state of Florida. How many members there are is not known, but it is estimated to be a few hundred independent Seminoles. These independent Seminoles live in very remote parts of the Everglades."

I thanked Mr. Peterson for the information and said to him, "Should we have further questions we would contact him again." Mr. Peterson promised to help in every way. We thanked him and left the casino, but not before we had a drink at the expense of the house.

The next morning, the names of the CDSF board were on my desk. This firm is an international holding company. Top members of the firm included:

Chairman: Dr. Nigel Pastor, Deputy: Sam Petrovich, Finance: Paul McRian. His Deputy is Dr. Ali Hussuf.

Then there were: Peter House (public relations). Dr. Han Sussy (architect and technical director of urban planning). And the two deceased, Chris Apples, he was a geologist, and Stan McPride, he was a member of the city planning team according to the company papers.

Bert found out that Dr. Nigel Pastor is said to have links to the Colombian Drug Mafia, but no proof yet. He has been monitored 24/7 by our Drug Enforcement team for over the past year, but with little success.

Dr. Nigel Pastor owns a mansion in Naples on Cordon Drive. Sam Petrovich, a born Russian with an American passport, is a billionaire. He lives in New York and makes his money from real estate and other bizarre business.

Financial Manager Paul McRian has not been noticed so far. Dr. Ali Hussuf, is an investor from Abu Dhabi. He is in possession of a valid residence permit. His business and behavior showed no signs of suspicius activities. The same can be said of Peter House and the two dead men, Stan McPride and Chris Apples. Chris Apples was a geologist and Stan McPride was the city planner. Dr. Han Sussy is an architect and so far he has shown no suspiciuos activities.

I was surprised that our institutions, such as the FBI, CIA, NSA, did not notice the plans and activities of the CDSF, were they too small fish? It concerns public land

and I think that alone is sufficient to examine the activities of the "company" in more detail.

I believe the Everglades need to be preserved with all available means to protect it from any interference with this unique Eco-system. We owe this to our fellow citizens and all subsequent generations. So, I'm surprised that such a plan to build a new Las Vegas in a conservation area has gone unnoticed to this day. Normally, something seeps through quickly, especially to the press, which always has a sense for such news. The press, and also the FBI, have only become aware because of the accident and the deaths of Mr. McPride, Mr. Apples and the Miccosukee scout Osceola, in the Everglades. Also, I think, we owe it to the few remaining Indian clans, to deal extensively with this mysterious company. The very idea of pure avarice, consciously destroying the Everglades is highly criminal.

Our government did not treat the Indians well during the Seminole war and after; instead they were treated in a very inhumane way. They have been persecuted aggressively and cold-heartedly. The governmnent forced the clans to retreat to the remotest corners of the Everglades. That is a dark side of our history, unfortunately!

I asked myself who could stand behind the deaths of the three men in the Everglades? Could the independent tribes be involved? I asked my colleagues. We need anwers. Snake proposed to pay a visit to the independent Seminole and Miccosukee.

"Have you ever made a trip deep into the Everglades? I do not mean the tourist paths either. It will not be easy even for me! It is not completely free of risk," Snake asked. "No," I said. Bert shook his head negatively, "We haven't yet," he replied, "But sounds like a challenge and adventure. Let's tackle that after we've checked out the CDSF company."

"Think twice," cautioned Snake, we'll have to do it all by airboat, canoe and the rest on foot. I'll ask my clan to hold a pow wow for us, so the River of Grass is well minded." Bert and I laughed and Snake exclaimed, *"I'm serious!"* We could do it with a helicopter, but I think you two should get a better idea of our habitat, a relationship, to this unique nature. He contiued, "Let me prepare this, I first have to ask some clan members where we can find the independent Seminole tribes."

The next day we stepped on the entrance mat at CDSF in Miami. We were escorted to a feudal looking meeting room by the secretary and asked to sit down. The deputy chairman, Sam Petrovich, would talk to us immediately, but he was in an important meeting, it would not be too long.

The secretary offered us a coffee, but we declined with thanks, then she disappeared, smiling, towards her office. Ten minutes later we were greeted by Sam Petrovich. He apologized for making us wait so long, but the meeting was extremely important and urgent, he said. He asked what he could do for us. We put our FBI badges on the huge boardroom table and asked for information about the dead peoble in the Everglades, specifically what the exact assignment of the CDSF members in the Everglades was.

Next, we wanted to learn more about the plan of a city on the reservation. Which offices have been informed so far, if at all? Are permits requested, etc? Where exactly should the city arise? Are there or were there talks with the tribes? Who were the conversation partners?

The man with the Russian accent, Sam Petrovich, appeared very calm and in a soft voice he began to comment on the questions.

"First of all, Chris Apples and Stan McPride, had the task to investigate the soil conditions of the Everglades in more detail." He tried to explain to us that this was very important to build high-rise buildings in such difficult terrain because you had to know the soil conditions very well. Most of the planned skyscrapers would have to be built on stilts, which are rammed deep into the ground. This type of engineering had been used in the construction of Dubai's buildings and you could use this here in the Everglades too.

To determine this, we had sent the geologist and the city planner with echo sounders and other geological instruments into the Everglades.

I took notes because no such instruments were found anywhere. It looks like we'll have to search again. I told him that these instruments hadn't been found, neither on the boat nor at the sites of the dead people. Very strange!

He went on to say that the relevant offices are working on the permits, but he cannot say which official bodies are involved. He can find out and then lets me know who the planners are currently working with. I told him, "Please do that, it would help us a lot."

Mr. Petrovich continued, "To answer your question as to whether we have connections with the Seminoles and the Miccosukee Tribes, yes, we have. That's not a criminal offense, is it?" "No", I answered, "that is not, but the establishment of a city in the reserves, yes it is". The reserves of the Seminole/Miccosukee are public lands and are under the strict protection of the state.

He replied, "The gain of such a metropolis, between Naples and Miami, would make economical sense. The exploding tourism would lead the Indians to unbelievable wealth. The CDSF will do everything possible to minimize the impact on the ecosystem. If you want, I can show you that model. You will be astonished!" he proudly stated.

Together we went to a large conference room, where in fact, the model of an ultramodern city was displayed. It took our breath away, it was gigantic! It was designed in the style of Dubai and Abu Dhabi.

Most of the skyscrapers stood on stilts, interconnected with glass tubes and bridges, it looked like something from another world. Mr. Petrovich further stated that the US 41 would be upgraded to an eight-lane Inter-State. Within the city, traffic is handled by high-speed monorails. This will, of course, be available free of charge to visitors. There will also be waterways, such as the canals in Cape Coral with corresponding water taxis, which will also be free to use. Further planning envisions using autonomous flying air taxis. All the individual traffic will be electric cars. The casinos are networked with each other through these traffic systems. Currently, about 100 casinos are planned.

When asked how big the available space would be, Mr. Petrovich replied, "Las Vegas measures 135.9 square miles, and about the same is needed for Miccosukee City.

It will about 20 miles west to east and 30 miles north to south. From Marco Island, the center is 40 miles east and about 37 miles west of the Miccosukee Resort."

I replied, "This is a huge area in the heart of the Everglades, that would mean the immediate death of the whole area, but the thought of it is so absurd! "I'm sorry," I said harshly, "But I'm sure that will never be approved! The model looks beautiful, but they have chosen the wrong place for it." Sam Petrovich answered, "You may think so but you have no control over the decision. Decisions regarding building are made in much higher circles, you have nothing to do with it, nothing at all.

"Now I would like to ask you to leave our company, I have even more important appointments to do unless you still have further reasons to keep me from my work, please, this way gentlemen," he showed us the way to the door, bowed and disappeared through the back glass door.

"Holy crap what a pompous man!" exclaimed Snake, "That was an award winning performance. He made the impression as if he was in the better position. His behavior alone should spur us to dig deeper into the tooth."

"We may have stumbled into a wasp nest," I said, "We should take care of ourselves from now on, we can't trust them at all. There is too much money in the game, which is enough to give some people bad ideas." I warned everyone. "So, people take care of yourself. Whenever possible, we act together and everyone pays attention to the back of his colleague. Is that clear?"

"Okay, boss," it sounded simultaneously from both throats. "I don't want to paint the devil on the wall, but better safe than sorry. Keep your weapons handy. Now let's go back, it's already late. We'll discuss the further procedures tomorrow morning in the office."

Snake did the driving and it took us nearly two hours to get to Fort Myers. During the ride we mainly discussed the arrogant appearance of Mr. Sam Petrovich and how it made us laugh.

The next morning, in the office, we arranged for the review of the individual members of the CDSF Board of Directors. I instructed the individual departments to take care of the monitoring and keep me up-to-date. I always wanted to know what was going on with that company.

I decided to investigate Dr. Nigel Pastor the chairman, a bit deeper. Naples Gordon Drive is not too far from Fort Myers. Bert, Snake and I went to take a closer look at Dr. Nigel Pastors mansion.

Snake and Bert were supposed to watch the front area, I wanted to approach from the beach side of the property. I had brought with me my little helper, a drone with a high-resolution camera. The entire property was difficult too see. Everything was surrounded by a six foot high fence and even higher plants. Why someone would obstructs his view of the sea with high fences is a mystery to me. There has to be a reason for it.

The entrance was a huge artistically designed iron gate, with guard houses left and right, with the appropriate guards occupied. The gate was only opened when one of the guards signaled to the other by a show of hands that the visitor was logged in. What a hassle to secure a private house. This could not be observed at any other house on Gordon Drive. Already strange.

I took a side street with access to the Gulf of Mexico and strolled along the beach, heading south. There were only a few tourists on the beach. Some homeowners were enjoying the nice afternoon by lying out and letting the sunshine on there bellies. We from the FBI cannot afford that, I thought.

When I arrived at the estate, of Dr. Nigel Pastor, I unpacked my little drone. Snake and Bert reported that just then four black limousines, with dark glazed windows, had driven up. The guards let them in immediately through the sliding gate. Snake commented that they were probably already expected.

My flying eye was ready to take off and I steered the drone vertically, about 150 feet in the air. The camera immediately began to record everything; I could see on my iPad that the five limousines Snake told us about stoped on the semicircular driveway. There were a lot of guards running around the building with submachine guns at the ready. "Oops," I said to myself, that looks like a summit meeting, and I don't think they want visitors and witnesses at the meeting. I was probably right, two ATV's approached. The vehicles came through the sliding door just opened in the fence and headed straight for me. I just had seconds to inform Bert and Snake.

There were broad-shouldered looking men dressed in black suits and dark sunglasses already approaching me. The first one asked me in an urgent voice, what I was doing there and told me I was on privately owned grounds. The owner absolutely does not want any recordings of his possessions and I should give him the made recordings of the drone immediately. He had his right hand under his jacket and I could see the imprint of a pistol. I stayed cool and explained to him that he was probably misinformed because I was still on public land. As everyone knows, the beach is public, from the waterline to the high tide line. In addition, I did not take pictures of the property but filmed the beautiful sunset and the beach and that is not forbidden.

The second man got off his ATV and said that I shouldn't make any trouble and just hand him over the required material, he also had his weapon under his suit in his hand.

Out of the corner of my eye, I saw Bert hiding behind a bush. He had his weapon ready and I thought, Snake is certainly also on the lookout. I said in a demanding voice to the two, "FBI! Take your weapons very slowly from your holsters and throw them in the sand, I seldom repeat myself!" I knew what was coming, the two of them turned and tore their weapons out of the holsters, that was stupid because bullets flew from two directions at the same time at them. The man on the ATV was hit and blown from his seat immediately and the man closest to me fell down and held his left leg, the sand on the beach slowly turned crimson from the blood flowing out. The ATV man lay in the sand and wailed terribly.

I called to Bert and Snake, take the ATVs and let's get out of here before the whole pack is after us. I collected my drone, which held its position all the way through, it automatically does that as soon as I let go of the controls. Bert and Snake sprinted over and we sat down with the ATV's and headed north.

I sat behind Bert and called over the radio to our office to call the Naples Police Department to take care of the matter. Our colleagues confirmed my call and said that a SWAT team was already on its way. A team of Drug Enforcement Agents, (DEA) was on the spot anyway, they had already moved on the property.

We raced the ATVs to our parked car and left the inhospitable scene. On the way, we received the news that everyone on the property was arrested. Only a limousine was able to escape before the teams seized everyone. The sedan was spotted on a side street, not far from Naples Airport, the driver was found dead with a gunshot wound to his head.

Now, all the chickens were startled, because these were no small offenses anymore, we suddenly had to deal with organized crime.

Back in our department, there was a lot of excitement! There were agents in the office, which I had never seen before, even our boss was present! And he also gave me a reprimand, he said, that was close. Our Boss told us, "I want you to coordinate with the other agencies and departments. No more running your own investigation! Got that?" "Yes Boss," I replied coolly.

The drug people have complained that they were not informed of our mission. But at the same time they said, with our appearance, they would have had to intervene and would have made a great catch. A total of 17 suspects were arrested. Including diplomats from Colombia. In addition, millions of dollars' worth of drugs were confiscated. Overall, a great success. Only the homeowner escaped the Drug Agents and SWAT team. This would have been the limousine that drove away.

My boss granted us special permits to help in the further handling of the company CDSF and the tribes. From now on, all means of transport, including the special weapons of the FBI, were available to us. We were always able to request help from the other special departments (special agents). For as long as I've been working at the FBI, that has not happened before. We have caused a great stir, especially in the drug scene.

It was very late when I drove home. From now on, the office would be staffed around the clock with agents from our head office in Sarasota. All individual missions were now controlled by them.

That night, I was torn from sleep with the ring of my phone. I looked at my clock, I had barely been sleeping for an hour. It was the office calling to let me know that a Learjet crash was reported in the middle of the Everglades. The suspicion is obvious that a connection with the escaped limousine exists.

The aircraft's registration was N-CDSF owned by the company, CDSF. Everything was fitting together. Where exactly the crash site is, is not known. Miami ATC (Air Traffic Control) lost contact with the private jet about 20 minutes ago. They assumed a crash had occurred. The Learjet 45XR aircraft took off from Naples Airport and had filed a flight plan for Cali Colombia. The flight plan passed over Miles City, then south direct to Marathon Key, continuing on to Cienfuegos Cuba, then over Cayman Island to the Airport Alfonso Bonilla Aragon (Cali). The flight time was given as 3 hours 39 minutes, at an altitude of 42000 feet (FL420). The flight was followed by ATC radar until after the intersection DEEDS. Then the plane turned, according to the flight plan, to the south on a course of 183 degrees. Then suddenly it disappeared from the radar according to the tracking done by Miami Radar.

At the time of the disappearance, it had a flight altitude of 12,000 feet and was cleared by ATC for FL320 (32,000 feet). The aircraft was on the climb to the required height. The radar controllers reported a sudden loss of altitude after reaching a height of 18,000 feet and at 1,000 feet it had disappeared from the radar and no radio contact could be made. The air traffic control then immediately alerted the emergency services.

We were alerted almost simultaneously to the disappearance of the Learjet. I felt the urge to call my two colleagues, Bert and Snake, but I let it go because the news was not so urgent that it couldn't wait until tomorrow morning.

I informed the office and let them know that I would visit Naples Airport in the morning. I turned around and immediately fell asleep again.

In the morning Bert, Snake and I met at Naples Airport and asked the FBO (fixed base operator) of the airport who had handled the flight of the Learjet with the registration # N-CDSF last night.

We also wanted to know who was responsible for the maintenance of the aircraft and whether the aircraft was based at the airport.

The FBO manager confirmed that the jet was stationed here at Naples Airport, but also had its own hangar at the Miami Opa Locka Executive Airport. Further, the aircraft would have a maintenance contract with the Naples Jet Center. For major inspections and maintenance events, there is a contract with Eagle Creek Aviation Service.

We thanked him but wanted to talk to the line maintenance service mechanic, who had handled the flight. The manager gave us his name, Alex van der Gard. "He's just finishing an Aircraft," the Manager told us. "I'll go tell him to come to the office so you can interrogate him."

"Nobody wants to interrogate anyone," I said, "We just want information about yesterday's flight." "Okay," the Manger replied, "I thought Alex might have had something to do with the crash." "Why do you think that?" I asked.

The manager replied, "Well, he was very disturbed last night and went straight home after his shift. He said he was not feeling well," the Manager stated.

"Oh that's interesting, did he tell you if he noticed something?" I asked.

"No, he didn't but his behavior was very strange, we are not used to that. He is always a happy guy and ready for all sorts of jokes, but not last night."

"Please leave us alone when we talk to him."

Alex came in the door and the manager tolded him, "These gentlemen would like to talk to you about the Learjet 45XR N-CDSF, which has been missing since last night," then he closed the door behind him and we were alone with Alex. He looked visibly nervous and he did not dare to look directly at us.

I introduced myself and my two colleagues and told him to tell us what happened last night. Alex said a man had come to him while preparing the plane for departure and said to him that the co-pilot had forgotten the folder of the flight manual at home. He would have taken the manual home for study but forgot to take it with him for this flight. "The guy asked me to put the manual in the side pocket of his co-pilot's seat," explained Alex. "He introduced himself to me as Peter and he was the brother of Jeff the co-pilot. He said that his brother called him by phone to pick up the manual at home and deliver it to the Airport, Jeff told him that he needed the papers urgently for the flight."

Alex continued, "Then the man laughingly said goodbye to him and said that I should greet his brother and wish him a good flight." Alex said he put the flight manual in the side pocket of the co-pilot's seat but forgot to address the co-pilot.

He regrets the disregard of the rule. To his apology, he said it was already very late and he had a stressful day, so he forgot. "Okay," I said to him, "Just one more question. According to the flight plan, 6 persons were on board, can you confirm this?" "No," he said, He could not, because after refueling he had only briefly talked to the crew, but he had not looked into the cabin and counted the passengers. He saw a limousine drive up while refueling, but did not how many people actually got on the plane because he was busy refueling.

A few minutes later, a "follow-me" car of the airport with the two pilots pulled up. They would have shown him the prescribed customs and immigration papers. Yes, he remembers now, there were 6 people in the flight plan, the 2 pilots, and 4 passengers.

Alex also informed us that twenty minutes after takeoff, he had remembered the manual and he tried to reach the aircraft via radio, but he was unable to contact the aircraft. Afterward, he had gone home with a guilty conscience.

Just this morning, he learned from his manager that the Learjet was missing over the Everglades.

"Okay," I said, "That's all for today."

At the moment it is not possible to speak clearly about a crash, the plane has to be found first. If it really did crash, no one can release you from a partial guilt. I imagine the crash site will not be that easy to find. We left the young man alone.

We made our way to the Naples Jet Center to see the technical documentation of the Lear 45XR, just so we get an overview of whether the jet had complied with the prescribed checks. With the documents, there was nothing to complain about, the Learjet 45XR was reported airworthy and had all the necessary certificates. The National Transportation Safety Board (NTSB) will certainly take a closer look at the documentation.

The NTSB is the department responsible for aviation accident investigations.

After we finished at the Naples Jet Center we drove back to the office. Maybe they already have new insights. "What's the latest in the search?" I asked the team. "Nothing yet Phil," replied one of the agents. "We're still feverishly looking for the jet."

My cell phone rang, it was Alex from Naples Airport. He said he had forgotten to mention that the limousine belonged to the same company as the plane, so the "brother" had a code for the gate, without the code no one can enter the airfield. "Thanks for the information," I said, "That's very interesting and takes us one step further, if you have any ideas, call me."

It's already been 14 hours since the jet disappeared and still no evidence of the crash site. It's as though the plane's remains had been swallowed up by the swamp.

Snake said to us, "Can you remember the crash of ValuJet; I think it was 1996. The DC-9 with the flight number 592 crashed a few minutes after takeoff from Miami International into the Everglades."

Bert and I also remembered that tragic day, "I believe there were 104 passengers and 5 crew members killed," I said. After the crash site was found, considerable efforts had to be made to recover the aircraft. The plane was buried under 25 feet (about 8 meters) of mud. It was extremely difficult even get to the plane. The rescue work was interrupted frequently by alligators and snakes. The reptiles had to be removed from the crash area first, so the rescue team could work without fear. The crash site was only accessible by airboat and helicopter.

It took a week to get to the main wreck, the entire area around the wreck had to be drained first. This means 25 feet of mud, as thick as molasses, had to be removed. An extremely difficult task. Well, I imagine it will be no less difficult to find the Learjet 45XR. Because it is not even half the size of the DC-9, so it is quite possible that the wreck was totally swallowed by the swamp.

In the afternoon, the NTSB informed us that, despite the intensive search, there was no evidence of a crash, no debris, absolutely nothing. The NTSB had requested a helicopter with special equipment. The helicopter from Dallas was already on the way. On it rested the hopes that the wreckage and survivors, if any, will be found. It would be a miracle if someone survived the crash.

Two days later, I received the message that indeed the wreck had finally been found. As expected, it was buried two yards deep under thick mud. As with the ValuJet crash, the entire area around the wreck must be drained to allow the rescue teams to approach the plane. The helicopter with the special radar discovered the wreck only by accident. The largest parts would be the engines of the jet. The GPS data of the crash site was: 25 ° 35'12.25 "N 80 ° 56'21.51" W. "That does not sound very hopeful," I said to my partners, "Should we go to the site? Or should we wait until they have found and identified people?" "Let's wait until we have names," Bert and Snake chimed in. "Okay," I said, "Let's wait. What can we do in the meantime?" Snake reminded us that we had wanted to pay a visit to the independent Seminoles anyway. We decied now is the right time and we could drop by the crash site on the way to get an idea of what it looked like. Another thing we need to do is, visit the company CDSF and find out about the "brother." And why did he have the company car at the Naples airport on the evening of the disappearance of the company jet. "Then let's go to Miami," I said, "The Seminoles can wait. I think they have the least to do with those dead in the Everglades, although they have every reason to do something against the blueprint of CDSF.

Snake swung behind the wheel and off we went. We were traveling on Interstate-75 in the direction of Miami. Halfway there we saw a lot of helicopters and other planes heading south of I-75. "That probably marks the crash site," Bert said, "There's a lot going on." We saw helicopters on and off while we drove. There were even larger transport helicopters, carrying heavy loads, as we could see from a distance.

We approached the CDSF headquarters and entered the foyer and went straight to the front desk. The pretty blonde, at the desk asked politely if we were registered and whom we would like to see. I put my ID on the table in front of her and said to answer her question, "No we are not logged in yet, we would like to speak to someone on the board." The pretty blonde replied that this was not possible at the moment, as all the gentlemen were out of the building and she didn't know when someone would be back. "Oh, that's interesting," said Snake, "How long have the gentlemen been out?" The blonde curly receptionist answered that she had not seen any of the gentlemen for three days. "It must have something to do with the disappearance of the company plane," she added. I asked her, "How she came to that conclusion. "Each of the gentlemen were very excited when they learned of the disappearance and possible crash," she exlpained, "Only Mr. Petrovich held back his feelings so we couldn't see how hard the crash hit him. He was very much in control," she said. All employees are still very affected by the news.

I asked, who of the gentlemen was aboard the plane? "As far as I know, Dr. Nigel Pastor and Financial Manager Paul McRian were supposed to be on board," she answered. "The gentlemen had mentioned the day before that they would fly to Colombia for a week," the woman added. I gave my business card to the blonde and asked her to call me immediately when someone from the executive suite checks in. She promised to do so immediately. We thanked her and left the office.

Back on the I-75, it happened. A black sedan with dark glazed windows began ramming us from behind at high speeds! It started pushing us from the interstate into the right side channel which is a trench filled with water. Only the attention of Snake's driving skills do we owe that we didn't land in there and we're still alive. We had overturned and landed on the roof of the car. "Is anyone hurt," I asked a bit dizzy, both answered, "No, they're okay."

"What the hell was that? Somebody must be mad at us, after our visit to the company CDSF," supposed Snake. "I saw the limousine approaching but it was already too late to get out of the way, they were traveling pretty fast!" We called over the radio to our State Trooper colleagues and reported on the attempted murder on us. We gave a description of the sedan and hoped that the colleagues could stop the fleeing vehicle in time. I requested a replacement car to pick us up and bring us to the Miccosukee Indian Casino. I said to my two colleagues,

"Let's check if anyone is missing from the Miccosukee General Council, especially from the Building Department or someone from the Council itself. I have such a suspicion."

The replacement car arrived 20 minutes later, along with the tow truck, which piggybacked our damaged vehicle. By now, five Highway Patrol Cars had arrived, including ambulances. They were eager to take us to a hospital for an examination. We said thankfully, that none of us were injured, at least not so hard that we needed to go to the hospital. I had received a small laceration on my head, which was immediately taken care of by the paramedics. We took over the new car and the Miami colleagues asked us, if possible, return our beautiful new car in one piece, please! We promised to do what we could but we couldn't promise anything because there are so many bad boys on the streets. Everyone laughed, then we drove to the Miccosukee Casino.

The secretary at the Building Department did not even try to scare us, but recognized us and asked who we wanted to talk to. "Whoever is from the upper floor in the building," I said. She disappeared through the glass door and came back shortly after with Rob (Deer) Peterson on her skirt. Rob greeted us warmly and asked how he could help us. "You could help by telling us whether you have noticed anything unusual in the last few days, or if anyone is missing," I answered.

Rob said, "How did you know that our Chairman Jack (Eagle) Osceola has not been in the office for quite a few days? We have not made a missing person report yet, as Jack sometimes prefers to disappear in the wild for a few days. He uses this time to 'recharge his strength,' as he always says." "It was just an idea," I said, maybe my theory is confirmed.

"Are Jack (Eagle) Osceola and Will (Eagle) Osceola (the dead guide from the Everglades) related to each other?" I enquired. Rob replied, "Yes, they are brothers." All the bells and whistles were rigoing off in our heads. But I said nothing. Snake and Bert looked at me, they had also recognized immediately that there may be a connection with the Everglade's deaths. I turned to Rob and said, "As soon as Jack logs back, please call us." We left our numbers and drove back to the office.

In the office, we were informed about the progress of the accident site. The NTSB reports that it would be extremely difficult to get to the fuselage or what was left of it. The search is also complicated by the fact that it succumbs again and again to attacks of alligators and other wildlife, especially snakes. The Seminole Tribe has sent 20 Indian scouts to the crash site to prevent these attacks. Since then, the rescue crews are focusing on their work without having to constantly look out for wild animals.

About 150 smaller fragments of the aircraft and some personal clothes have been found so far. The NTSB, due to the very small fragments, suspects that the Airplane had already broken apart in the air. So far, no survivors have been found. The NTSB suspects an explosion on board the aircraft, only this would explain the widely scattered wreckage. That, in turn, would explain the encounter at Naples Airport, where Alex the plane mechanic was asked by the "brother" to put the forgotten manual in the co-pilot's side pocket of his seat, I thought to myself.

I arranged for the NTSB to be notified immediately of what we had discovered at Naples Airport on the night of the Learjet 45XR's disappearance.

Searching in the right direction will certainly help in the investigation. It is possible that not as Alex was told, the forgotten flight documents that were delivered wasn't the actual manual but a bomb, disguised as a flight manual. Such bombs usually work with a pressure dependent detonator, after reaching a preset cabin pressure height, the detonator is activated. The size of the Learjet does not need a big explosive force because the cabin is under pressure. The Learjet 45XR operates with a 9.5 PSI differential pressure, at a maximum altitude of 51000 feet. A small bomb is enough, to blow a hole in the fuselage. This inevitably leads to a crash. The plane breaks up in the air and crashes.

The next morning, when I was done shaving, my cell phone rang, it was Rob (Deer) Peterson, he was very agitated. He said there had been a burglary in the office that night. The office of Chairman Jack (Eagle) Osceola was devastated and his desk was broken. The burglars also tried to break the vault in his office but they failed. The vault was badly damaged but not open. "Rob," I said, "We will be in your office as soon as possible, have you already informed the Miccosukee Police Department?" Rob confirmed that the police had just arrived. "Okay, we are leaving immediately."

I called my two colleagues and described what I had just heard. Bert said he is already on his way to the office and Snake would go straight to the Miccosukee Casino. Since he was still at home, it would take him only five minutes to get to there. "See you at the casino," I said. "Bert and I will take the helicopter, it takes too long by car, I think we'll be there in about 40 minutes." I told Snake.

I called the helicopter and Bert and the helicopter arrived at the Fort Myers Field Office almost simultaneously. Already we were in the air and along I-75 towards Miami.

When we landed, Rob (Deer) Peterson and Snake were already in the parking lot waiting for us. We took the private elevator to the office of Chairman Jack (Eagle) Osceola.

The forensics colleagues were already working and it was the same scenario as on any crime scene, nothing new for us.

I asked Rob if he knew what was in the vault. He said no, he hadn't a clue what Jack was stowing in it. I asked Rob if he would agree to let us open the vault. Rob replied that he also wants to know what's in it. "The way it looks to me, there's something of importance that someone had been looking for and maybe it's still in the vault. We agree with you, so let us try."

I asked the forensics team if they had a vault specialist on the team, yes they did. He then started to open the vault, he said it would take at least 3-4 hours because this vault has two independent opening mechanisms. He contacted the manufacturer of the vault and they explained the technical features.

We figured we'd just get in the way, so we went to Rob's office. Rob seemed rather desperate, saying that Jack (Eagle) Osceola would always have tried to decide alone what was going on with the Miccosukee Council. For this, Jack has been questioned several times by the other members of the Council. He hopes that Jack isn't hiding anything unlawful in his safe. The secretary provided us with a sumptuous breakfast and we let it all happen. It was late afternoon when the safe specialist called us and said the vault was open, so we should come to the office.

Well, we are curious, as to what's in it, possibly, nothing at all, let's surprise ourselves. And we were surprised when we sorted the contents of the safe together! In addition to the normal business records, we found a building application signed by Jack (Eagle) Osceola to build a city in the reservation area of the Miccosukee tribe. Further, we found a special permit from the state of Florida, signed by the head of the Building Department Ray Hudson. "Wow," I said, "That's pretty tough, with these papers in the hands of CDSF, there might have been nothing to stop the city's construction. Immediately, I started a search for Deputy Chairman Sam Petrovich, Reason: Suspected blackmail, bribery, robbery, kidnapping, attempted murder, suspected of membership in a criminal organization. I think that's enough to take the man in custody.

We learned through a phone call from the NTSB that the work was progressing well. They had located a major part of the aircraft, possibly a part of the fuselage. So far, the pilots and Paul McRian's ID have been found, as well as a card from a Colombian state member named Salvador Rodrigues. "At the moment we are about to uncover the found piece of the hull," stated the NTSB agent, "In one or two hours we should know more."

We were waiting for the next news, when Bert had an idea. "Maybe we should fly to the crash site and get a picture of the crash. Then we could pay a visit to the independent Seminoles".

Snake and I agreed. Snake thought that would be worth it because from the crash site it would be about 9 miles to a group of independent Seminoles. The group had set up camp not too far from the crash site, he had learned that from his clan. "Okay," I said, "Let's do this."

Snake told us he would take care of the equipment that was urgently needed to get to the Seminoles' camp.

I took care of getting a helicopter to take us to the wreck site, and I also asked the NTSB team if we were even welcome. I got the green light from the team. Both of us, Bert and I were waiting for Snake, who was still busy putting together the equipment. An hour later, Snake called saying he had everything together and we could leave anytime. We agreed with the helicopter pilot that he should pick us up the next morning.

In the early morning, we met in the parking lot where the helicopter was supposed to pick us up. Bert and I were amazed when Snake showed up and unloaded his equipment. "For heaven's sake, do we need all this stuff?" I asked.

Snake replied, "You'll be glad for every piece of this equipment!"

We heard the helicopter, which landed immediately afterward in the secured parking lot. We already knew the pilot; he had already flown us to the casino in Miami. After a short welcome, we took off, in the direction of the discovery of the Learjet. Forty minutes later we reached the site. We immediately noticed that there was really something big going on! Excavators laid dry the swamp around the place of discovery and we now saw an aircraft body part about 9 feet long. It was torn open on the right side, only the left side seemed to be reasonably intact. We explained to the Heli Pilot what we planned to do and arranged a meeting place. Snake explained to him we would need 2-3 days to get to the camp of the Seminoles. Also, we agreed on an emergency code for our RF radios, if something should go wrong. A quick goodbye and he was back in the air; direction Page Field (KFMY).

The leader of the rescue force introduced himself and explained what was found so far. This was not very much but some finds clearly showed burn marks, the fragments were also clearly bent from inside to outside, this means, the inside was arched outwards. The NTSB specialist told us that is an indication of an explosion in the cockpit. The find was perfectly identified as a component of the right cockpit side. This explains the cause of the crash. I said to him, *"This is consistent with the statement of the mechanic at the airport in Naples, who had unknowingly placed a bomb in the cockpit."*

I wonder why someone blows up a plane, who benefits? Bert, Snake and I talked for a while about where the scene of the crash lies and why six people had to die. We did not come to a common denominator.

"Possible, as with many capital crimes, is the sickly greed for money and power," I said. Bert and Snake shared my opinion, pointing out that the search for Sam Petrovich was a right move. Unfortunately, so far without any success. Bert and Snake are of the opinion that Sam Petrovich is the mastermind, he is behind all this. But what was the motive?

Hopefully, he will soon get caught in the investigators' net so that we can ask him the right questions. I too, am of the same opinion, but we could be wrong, and are looking in the wrong direction. Maybe things are different, let's wait and see.

We stood from a distance, watching the activities of the NTSB people, who were getting bits and pieces out of the mud. They went very carefully, numbered the parts and tried to identify them by serial or part numbers. A rather tedious and sweaty job, Bert noticed. "Yes," I said, "The sweat is boiling in my buttocks too, this is unbelievable heat. How do the guys endure this unspeakable heat?"

Snake interjected and said, "We should get going before it gets dark, but I can tell you one thing now, it will not be much cooler at night either." "Well, Bravo, that's great prospects," said Bert. Have you brought any air conditioning for the tents? With the amount of gear you're taking along, you surely must have," joked Bert. Snake took it easy and laughed, "Of course, I won't carry the equipment alone, it will be divided nicely among us three. I saw it coming, I said, "What did I get involved with?" Snake, quipped, "Too late, you two agreed, now you have to go through with it." He grinned and enjoyed himself deliciously. "We will head south in

15 minutes. Please wear the long-sleeved shirts that I bought for you, and you should spray yourselves with the insect spray now, any area not covered."

Snake continued to inform us that today's stage won't be very difficult, that is to settle in. Bert muttered something to himself, but let it go. Snake distributed the equipment among us, but I noticed that he had stored much more than we had in his backpack.

We were just about to say goodbye to the NTSB people and leave, when the head of the crew came rushing to us shouting we should wait, they have made a find that will surely interest us. The guy wanted us to follow him to the hull. When we got there and saw what he was talking about, it blew us away in the truest sense. We stood there with incredulous looks on our faces and could not believe what we saw.

What the crew liberated from the mud was an almost intact aircraft seat and on the right armrest, the arm of a man was handcuffed.

It was quiet and the men stopped working, everyone stood in disbelief in front of the seat and shook their heads, even the die-hard NTSB men had not seen something like this before.

Horrible and unbelievable, a person dies handcuffed to a seat.

I asked if any items were found that might indicate the identity of the dead person.

"Yes," said one man, holding a piece of ID in his hands and he showed it to me. I could read fragments of a name, ..y .... Unreadable Chair ... illegible Florida .uild ... Com .... "This must be sent immediately to the forensics people," I ordered.

"I've already notified them of what we have found," replied the boss of the crew. "They are on the way." My two colleagues were still dazed and did not say a word.

Snake was the first to recover, "Why someone was abducted against his will and tied to the plane seat. Why a kidnapping?"

Who was the man or the woman? To our knowledge, six people were on board, now there were seven because the dead person was certainly not on the flight documents. "We won't know anything until clear identification, it will certainly take 3-4 days to get," said the NTSB boss.

Snake said, "Then we should leave now so that we can reach our destination before dark and build our tents. We can't do anything here anyway. We will only get in the way of recovery crew."

We shouldered our backpacks and headed south, Snake said we had just over three hours to go until sunset, we should make it to the Hardwood Hammock, which he had chosen for the night. Hardwood Hammocks are relatively dry elevations and densely wooded islets in the swamp, a tropical, shady forest, some of the forests are very small and others can be square miles in size.

"Okay, the distance for today is 2.5 miles, the compass direction is 199 degrees, we should be able to do that," Snake said, "If you don't mess up before. An experienced hiker, covers about 3 mls/h, we can make maybe 0.8 mls/h in this difficult terrain. With the heat comes all sorts of unforeseen complications." "Well, you're really encouraging us," I said, Bert muttered something to himself again, which nobody understood. Maybe that was better so too.

The strain begins! Snake told us to spray carefully with the mosquito spray, don't forget any spot, face, neck, hands, do not forget your fingers!

We were not yet a ¾ mile away, because we, the city people, had to take the first break, we were sweating from all pores. Snake was nothing to look at either. He waited patiently until we regained our strength, but then he urged us again and said, *"Let's go, gentlemen, we still have 1.8 miles ahead of us".*

We walked through rough terrain, bordered by grass and bushes, then trees, where a lot of birds had settled down. For the first time, we consciously heard the voices of the Everglades, a very special concert drama, and Snake tried to explain to us the individual voices of birds, reptiles and also the squawking of insects. For him, those were the voices he had known since his youth, for us it was a jumble of voices, and it was not exactly quiet. We had come here dry, but now we have soaking wet feet. That was unpleasant and we had to get used to it. Here, Bert and I had to praise Snake for insisting that we put on the water-impermeable Goretex shoes. Nevertheless, we had wet feet.

Snake always ran in front of us and kept turning around, as if he did not want to lose any of his chicks. After another hour, we had to take another break, Snake asked if we were fine, and reminded us that we should be drinking enough water. Due to the unaccustomed effort and the heat, we would lose a lot of fluids and minerals. He turned to me, and I immediately got a proper reprimand from him, I had my hat off. "Please keep your hats always on your head even if it seems so annoying, the mosquitoes are just waiting for it," he said sternly.

We were now on the last leg of the day and it was still a half a mile to the finish. We could already see the Hardwood Hammock, and the vegetation around us was getting denser and more impenetrable. It was a tedious move on the last 200 yards. Then we had done it, just in time, because the sun was almost down and conjured up a glowing sunset on the horizon in the west. That was terrific, it happened quite quickly and then the red fireball had disappeared between the Hardwood trees. Now we had to quickly set up our tents. By the time we finished it was already dark.

Snake said to us; "You stay here and be vigilant, I'll collect dry wood for the night, it shouldn't take too long and I'll stay within calling distance, Okay?" Okay, we'll hold the position here.

When the tents were finaly set up, I turned to Bert and was surprised to seet hat he held his Luger in his hand. "Did you hear that?" He said nervously. "What?" I asked. "Well, there was a sound like someone coughing," he replied. "No, I didn't. I hear a thousand noises, but there was no cough." Snake came out of the darkness, and said to Bert, "You're right, you heard a noise that sounded like a cough, but that was just an alligator," I jokingly told him to get out of here. He went along with the joke at first, but came back.

Snake lit a fire and we squatted around it and ate our canned menu that we brought. "Shall I tell you some more campfire stories before I sing you to sleep?" Snake grinned. "Oh yes, dear Snake, that would be great," we booth chuckeld. And Snake began to tell us one. "It's the story of the Little Frog - as originally told by Betty Mae Jumper."

"This story was told to me by my grandmother when I was a baby. "Where we lived the sounds in the woods were very important to us, we always asked," 'What is that noise?" Many times the reply to our question was a story like this:

The little green frog was sitting

on the edge of the water lilies. A big old hare came hopping up, approached the frog and said, '"Hello! Why are you sleeping?" "It's too good to sleep," replied the little green frog. "Wake up! Wake up! Insisted the hare.

"I have nothing to do right now," said the irritated little frog, but the old hare did not stop bothering him until the little frog got really angry and said to him, "I'll teach you something." So the little frog began to sing his funny little song, which he does to call the rain. Within a few minutes, the black cloud came and the wind began to blow. Then the rain came and soaked the old hare so much that it got cold and he ran home. Whenever you hear that the frogs are singing, you better be near shelters because they warn you that rain will be coming soon.

After Snake finished the tale I said "It was a nice story, but please turn off the radio now, I cannot possibly sleep with this babble." Snake replied, "This is only the beginning, wait until it gets really deep into the night." He was right it got even worse as time went on. I heard sounds that I'd never heard before in my life. The concert was called "A night in the Everglades, sung and played by the local residents". Snake told us. We decided it was time to retire to our tents and sleep. Snake offered to take the first watch. After 3 hours he'll wake me up for the second watch, then it would be Bert's turn until the sun comes up. I retired to my tent, I was exhausted from the hike so it didn't take long for me to fall asleep.

Snake woke me up, because it was my turn for the next watch. Pretty sleepy, I sat down by the fire and listened to the night. It is unbelievable how many voices and sounds are heard at night. But after a while, you get used to it. After two hours sitting by the fire and listening to every strange noise, I put my Walther PPK back in my holster, I had kept the weapon in my hands for the whole two hours. Now it was time for the change of guard and I woke Bert. As always, he muttered something to himself, it sounded like, "Right now I'm falling asleep, you have to wake me up." He squatted by the fire and I saw that he also pulled his automatic from his holster.

I woke up with the smell of fresh coffee in my nostrils. Bert and Snake had made breakfast; coffee, bacon and scrambled eggs. I asked Snake "Where did you get the eggs from?" "These are not fresh eggs, replied Snake, "That's Publix Eggbeater out of the plastic bag." After breakfast, we packed our tents and garbage. We took the garbage back to dispose it when we get back to civilization.

Immediately we were on the way again. Snake was, as always ahead, he had hit a course of 235 degrees on his compass and he said: "Today we have 8 miles' ahead of us to Camp Lonesome, where the Seminoles camped. I hope you didn't forget to spray yourselves. I don't want to hear any complaints, like, I'm totally bitten by the mosquitoes." Bert and I both replyed like little campers, "Yes, Chief Snake, we have sprayed ourselves."

Where we waded yesterday the water was to our ankles, now we ran knee-deep in the water for an hour, which was extremely exhausting and we made only slow progress. Again and again Snake stopped and watched the alligators in the shallow water, it seemed like he was communicating with the beasts before continuing.

I have to admit that both of us, Bert and I, are lost out here. We city people would not be able to survive even one day alone in the

Everglades, too large are the dangers that lurk everywhere. We have seen a variety of snakes, extremely poisonous and huge ones, such as pythons. (Pythons are not snakes that are naturally occurring here, they were abandoned by people who kept the animals as pets and they set them loose when they were too big). Neither one of us would have noticed them, if Snake had not caught our attention.

As we passed through a small hammock, Snake suddenly stopped dead, made no sound and pointed to a tree about ten yards away, and then we saw it too. It was a Florida panther looking out from a branch of a cypress tree. He was difficult to see and I'm sure we wouldn't have even noticed him. Snake's alert eyes and innate instincts immediately noticed the panther. Snake said to us after we walked away very slowly, "You are one of the very few people who has seen a Florida panther in the wild, this is an extremely rare event. There are only 20 specimens living in the Everglades National Park where we are right now".

We crossed the hammock and waded back through the water, but now we were up to our hips and we had to carry our backpacks over our heads. We trudged through an area of cypress and hardwood trees. It was like moving in another world, seeing wild orchids in the trees, an incredible number of waterfowl, including cormorants, anhingas, ibis, snowy egrets, bald eagles, osprey, tricolored herons, and many other species. Snake knew them all by name. We had our second day's free lessons and learned from an Native American how to survive in the Everglades.

"Another hour," Snake said, "Then we are at Camp Lonesome, I'm proud of you!" After another 20 minutes he stopped again and said. "We have visitors, I can feel them. "Who can you feel," I asked. He told me that they are very close and watching us. Then he called something in his language and he was answered immediately. That's unbelievable, I've never seen, or heard that before, unbelievable. Now three of the Indians came out of their hiding places and approached us slowly. They greeted, Snake first, then us. Both of us, Bert and I did not understand a word they spoke. The older of the three had a conversation with Snake, he translated what was said. They wanted to know if we were the FBI people and if he could trust us. Snake said to him, he would put his hand in the fire for us, that seemed to satisfy the older one. The older man let us know, however, that he has no confidence in government officials, but he'll make an exception for us. Snake, said, *"You can be proud of that."*

The spell was broken, the tribe's chief now led the troop. I said softly to Bert, "I wouldn't like to meet him alone in the Everglades." Snake, who had heard that too, told us he looks terrifying, but he was a respected chief.

In the evening, we, Chief Sam (Jumper) Obiaka and some of his clan sat together in a circle in his "chickee". We ate roast venison with wild rice and mushrooms.

("Chickee" is a Seminole's house type covered with palm straw and the side walls open. On a platform inside, the inhabitants worked and slept.)

Our "Palaver" lasted until well after sunset, everything was discussed and my questions were answered by Chief Sam (Jumper) after being translated by Snake.

The Chief knew of plans to build a city on the reserve. He told us that would never happen because he would see that as a declaration of war and what that means ..., he was silent for a while, then he continued, "Probably it would be the end of the Seminole Tribes, but they have no choice. But you can be sure that all Tribes would follow my call." Then Chief Jumper broke off the palaver.

We stayed in a guest "chickee" for the night and I talked with Snake and Bert for quite a while. We came to the conclusion that the independent Seminoles had absolutely nothing to do with the deaths in the Everglades.

I said to my colleagues that I fully understand the point of view of Chief Sam (Jumper) and that the right is on his side, including me. Snake said fimly, "We must put a stop to CDSF's business before any further mischief is done." Okay, let's call the helicopter tomorrow morning to pick us up. Then we fell asleep.

The helicopter landed and it drew a huge crowd. The Indian children hopped around it with pure joy, I suspect they had never seen a helicopter before.

Chief Jumper chased away the children, said goodbye. We got into the Chopper, we took off and were on our way to Fort Myers' Page Field. The pilot could not resist saying, "My God, what have they done to you! You guys are totally bitten, red as lobsters and the smell is awful too. Please leave the window open a crack." "We can't laugh about that at all, just fly a bit faster so we can get home quickly and take a shower." Arriving home, I looked in the mirror and found, the helicopter pilot was right. Sunburn on the nose, the mosquitos have left their marks and the clothes stink of a swamp! There is nothing like taking a shower after a long trek in the mud and water of the Everglades.

After the basic cleaning, I felt reborn and full of energy, so I called the office and wanted to know the latest status on investigation. I have been informed, no success in the search, so far, but there was evidence of the stay of Peter House (responsible for public relations of the company CDSF). As soon as something happens I would be notified immediately. I met Bert and Snake for lunch at Grimaldi's

Pizzeria in Fort Myers located in the Bell Tower Shops. We were discussing our next steps, as the events unfolded. Just as we were finishing our pizzas, my phone rang. The office was calling to let me know that the wanted Peter House had been arrested a few minutes ago. We should come to the Fort Myers Police Department if we wanted to be present at the hearing. Of course, we wanted to! We had finished with our pizzas anyway and got ready to pay.

On the way to the police department, we got a second call, it was the forensic team, which told us that the person whose arm was handcuffed to the seat, was identified. His name is Ray Hudson, Chairmen of the Florida Building

Commission. I said "That's something, they kidnapped him, but what was the reason for it? Okay, let's talk about that later, first let's take a look at CDSF's Public Relation Man." We watched the initial interrogation by our Fort Myers colleagues, behind a mirrored glass window, we could not be seen from the inside. Our Police Department colleagues interviewed him first about his person, then about his position within the company CDSF. Mr. House was willing to provide information about the questions asked, but when asked about the deaths in the Everglades, he was stupid, you could tell he was nervous.

From this point on, we replaced the colleagues from the Police Department and took over the interrogation. We would not give up and we told him we had proof that someone in the company had his hands on it. Further I told him, we already have a confession from Dr. Han Sussy, regarding the Bomb, which crashed the company Learjet, so he had to stop lying, and then he fell into my trap. He yelled at me and said that's all a lie, because Han Sussy was murdered by Sam Petrovich, so he can't say anything anymore, "That's interesting" I said, and then he noticed his mistake and collapsed. From now on, Mr. House answered everything we wanted to know. Petrovich also threatened to kill Mr. House if he did not work with him. "He promised me three million dollars once everything was done." He watched as Petrovich shot Dr. Han Sussy because he refused to go on.

Mr. House said he'd been terrified and agreed to co-operate. He pleaded with us hoping we'd understand that Petrovich was "Extremely dangerous and ready for anything," he said. He had done nothing wrong and he was silent because of fear.

Petrovich staged the crash because Dr. Nigel Pastor realized that the city and casino would never come to construction because too many people were shaken up. Dr. Pastor wanted to move to Colombia and wanted to dissolve the company. Petrovich agreed with that and he promised Dr. Pastor that he would follow him, but first, he would have to secure the company's accounts and the cash from the drug deals. Petrovich would transfer the accounts from the Caribbean banks to Colombia into Nigel Pastor's account.

Dr. Pastor invited the Chairman of the Seminole Tribes, Jack Osceola, and the Chairman of the Florida Building Commission, he forgot the name, to his villa in Naples. He wanted to inform all those involved in the demolition of the construction project. Something must have happened in the villa because the flight to Colombia was planned for the next day. What happened at the villa, House didn't know, he had left immediately for Louisiana after Sam Petrovich had informed him about the hasty departure of Nigel Pastor from his villa.

Mr. House talked like an open book, we did not really need to ask questions, he actually provided us with everything we previously suspected.

Snake, asked him if he knew what had happened in the Everglades. He did not know the exact details, but he learned that Petrovich sent the two camouflaged professional killers, Stan McPride and Chris Apples to the Everglades to kill the brother of Chairman Jack (Eagle) Osceola, "I think his name was Will, he was an Airboat Captain from Everglades City. He was to be murdered to pressure Jack to sign the papers, which Jack did after learning of his brother's death." House informed us. He only learned about the deaths of the two killers through the press.

I asked what the Chairman of the Florida Building Commission has to do with all this. Peter House also had an answer for that, "The Chairman, I think his name is Ray Hudson, was bribed with millions of dollars and then blackmailed by Petrovich to sign the building permit. Petrovich was furious because Jack (Eagle) Osceola had locked the signed documents into his vault and had not delivered them to Petrovich as agreed." Slowly we got a picture of the processes and machinations of the company CDSF and Sam Petrovich. "What do you know about the whereabouts of Dr. Ali Hussuf?" I asked. "Ali has dropped off, I believe, to Syria, I have not heard from him ever since, responded House.

Finally, I wanted to know from him where Sam Petrovich is currently. He said he doesn't know, but he suspects that Petrovich is hiding out with Russian friends, where exactly, he doesn't know. "Okay," I said, "You are under arrest for membership of a criminal organization and for murder in at least two cases because of your own complicity."

I told my colleagues from the Fort Myers Police, who were standing behind the mirror and heard everything, to come take the arrested prisoner away. Snake, then said to me "You are a very cunning dog, to lure the poor guy on the ice, I did not think that he fell for it, he has fallen fully in your trap. Bravo!"

We informed our office and reported on the interrogation and asked for the current state of the search for Sam Petrovich. The colleagues at headquarters said they did not have a trace, then maybe I have one, I said. "It's possible that he is hiding with Russian friends, check all persons with a Russian background in Florida". The FBI should also expand the search to the southern states. The three of us were fully satisfied with today and we drove home.

I mixed a drink and leaned back in my favorite chair. I reviewed the knowledge gained and made a mental picture in my mind of what had happened on the airboat.

The two killers, Stan and Chris, disguised as geo-scientists and city planners, had brought the Airboat Captain on a pretext to stop the boat. The boat stopped and Will (Eagle) left his helm and came to the front, where the two pointed to something, he was overwhelmed by the two and one of the two injected the snake venom into his left arm. Will, was able to free himself and it came to a fight, he made it back into his helm and accelerated, the boat speeded up and through wild lurching movements, he tried to throw the two off the boat. The airboat had overturned, they were all thrown from the boat in a high arc, Will (Eagle) Osceola suffering a laceration at the back of his head during this time.

The gangsters fled south and Will pursued them for a while until he could feel the effect of the poison. Then he turned and ran back to the boat. He didn't make it, dying shortly before reaching the boat.

The two gangsters must have exhausted themselves during the escape so that they were completely at the end of their strength, the mosquitos and the sun did the rest. Presumably, they were so exhausted that they could no longer free themselves from the creepers into which they had become entangled. Bert and I had learned first-hand how challenging and difficult it is to move in the swamps. If someone tries to be quick, his power reserves are used up in no time. The two killers had just managed to cover a distance of one mile trying to escape. This is how I envisioned what had happened. Maybe it's right, maybe it's very different. It will probably never be completely cleared up.

I wrote my thoughts down on a piece of paper, so I won't forget it. I want to be sure mention everything in my daily report.

Bert and I met in the office the next morning, it was a relaxed but tense atmosphere. The staff was sitting at their computers and the oversized screens were constantly displaying information from various surveillance cameras. Our boss was in the midst of coordinating the hustle and bustle, he noticed us, approached us and said he just got some information from one of our agents. "Get on the way and check it," he ordered. He handed us a piece of paper with the data of the object to be checked.

The agent had observed that something was going on around this property, people were loading a speedboat with what seemed to him as food and other items. Some of the men wielded weapons, but he couldn't make it out clearly because the distance was too great, even through binoculars. The agent said he was sure enough to identify that the men were carrying machine guns. That was enough for our boss to rush us three to the described address.

We waited until Snake showed up in the office. After he appeared, we informed Snake of the agent's report. We expanded our arsenal to include assault rifles with night vision gear, and infrared aiming devices. I also packed my drone, you never know what it might be needed for. The drone always provides a good bird's eye view.

The address of the property is located on North Captiva Island and can only be reached by boat or plane, which of course makes the whole thing more difficult. We have to go to the Coast Guard Station at Fort Myers Beach so the boys can bring us with their speedboat to North Captiva, our office has already arranged that. When we got there, the crew was standing by and the boat was ready to leave.

The speedboat and its crew were armed to the teeth. The captain introduced himself and his crew and off we went. We talked to the captain about our plan and told him to drop us off at a place not too far from the given address. I just wanted to get an idea of what's going on, the Coast Guard crew should wait and see if we need them. We'd call them by radio if the situation demands it.

We turned and headed for Sanibel Island, south past the Sanibel Lighthouse. The boat kept a distance to Sanibel's coastline of three miles. It was just over 30 miles from the Coast Guard Jetty to North Captiva, the speedboat was over 55 knots (nautical miles) fast and we reached the west coast of North Captiva, 40 minutes later. We were dropped off at the North Captiva beach. From there to the specified address was 600 yards on foot.

The villa belonged to Anton Rasturev and is located at the north-eastern end of the Salty Approach Airstrip. The grass runway had a length of 710 yards. We reached a vacant lot, directly opposite the villa of Mr. Rasturev. The property was overgrown with palmetto palms and pine trees and provided excellent cover. On the opposite side, all sorts of things were happening, as we could observe through our binoculars.

On the east side of the house was a path leading to the jetty with two boats. It was almost loaded. The agent who gave the tip was right, at least four figures were running around with machine guns and guarding the loading of the speedboat.

The house had a huge garage door on its south side, probably an airplane hangar door.

We watched the action from our hiding place and saw that five men and a woman got on the boat and started the engine. The speedboat left the dock and headed for Cayo Costa and then presumably into the Gulf of Mexico. I informed the

Coast Guard crew, the boat should not be allowed to escape.

Bert quielty stated, "That is a pretty fast boat and in all likelihood would be tuned to maximum speed. such boats are used for the drug smuggling. I hope the Coast Guard can keep up with them."

Snake believed that the wanted Sam Petrovich was on board and trying to disappear in the direction of Mexico or Belize. I said, "We should wait and continue to watch the villa, I don't trust the ruse, as it looks, there are still the security guards in the house". Bert called for reinforcement back up via radio, I hoped that they would arrive on time. We decided to wait another half hour, then storm the villa and arrest the guards.

The Coast Guard captain informed us that he had picked up the pursuit of the speedboat, saying that the boat was heading southwest for at least 50 knots and that he had requested Coast Guard helicopters in case he was unable to catch up with the speedboat.

The volatile boat is at breakneck speed on the water, with the currently prevailing waves in the Gulf of Mexico it's bordering on suicide. The wave height is currently 6-8 feet. In the open Gulf the waves are predicted to be more than 12 feet. That is the maximum height for his ship with 55 knots to drive. The distance to the escaping boat is still ¾ of a mile and the distance is reduced by the minute, The captain expects that he will catch up with it in an hour, but fears that the escape boat will break up if it retains the speed in this swell.

The villa was quiet, no one was outside the building. We couldn't see what was going on in the house. We didn't know how many people really stayed in the house. Of course, this increases the risk of storming the villa before the reinforcements are here. We have just been informed that two boats and a helicopter with a 6-man crew still need about 15 minutes to be in the vicinity of the villa, the helicopter could be a few minutes earlier. We were still lying, waiting in our hiding place opposite the villa of Anton Rasturev and had decided to wait even longer, the risk was just too big to act on our own. At the moment there was nothing where we would have had to intervene.

Just before the half-hour, we noticed something was happening, the hangar door was being opened and an airplane was pushed out. It was a Cirrus SR 22 Turbo, as I could see it. A fairly fast machine with a range of over 1000 miles. That reaches to Central America, at least. And now I could clearly see through the binoculars, it was Sam Petrovich who climbed into the cockpit. Now we had to intervene, I blew for the attack and we stormed out of our hiding place, zigzagging over the runway to the plane. At the moment we were uncovered, we still had 20 yards, then we found cover again behind bushes and trees on the south side of the house. The guards immediatly discovered us and started shooting at us, the bullets flew around our ears and we shot back. One of the guards was hit by Snake, he fell and remained face down in the sand. I took out the second, Bert the third. The fourth took cover behind a barbecue cottage. Sam Petrovich was just starting the engine as the police helicopter approached from the east across the Pine Island Sound. I called the pilot over the radio, he should put the helicopter in the middle of the runway so that the aircraft has no way to takeoff. The pilot immediately recognized the situation and landed the helicopter on the runway, blocking the Cirrus SR22T from reaching it.

That was just in time, a few minutes later, and Sam Petrovich would have had escaped, so he was trapped for now. Petrovich had recognized the situation and jumped out of the plane, he fled back to the hangar, Bert and Snake chasing him down. He shot wildly around them now and the two had to seek shelter behind a lawnmower.

Meanwhile, the colleagues of the helicopter swarmed and surrounded the villa. The security guard who had entreched himself behind the barbecue house, came out with his hands raised from his hiding place. He had realized how pointless his situation was and surrendered. Snake, shouted to him to lie down on the floor with his hands behind his head, which he did. Snake handcuffed him and took him away.

Sam Petrovich had meanwhile fled back into the house. We consulted with our colleagues of the SWAT team on how to proceed. In the meantime, the two Coast Guard boats had arrived and occupied position around the house. I asked Sam Petrovich over loudspeakers to surrender, the house was surrounded and he had no chance to escape, I said, he should come out with his hands up, or the house would be stormed. Five minutes later, there was an explosion, the Pine Island Sound shook. Sam Petrovich had blown himself up. The inglorious end of a criminal. He preferred to die rather than face charges.

The captain of the Coast Guard speedboat reported that the escaping boat was upset, that the Coast Guard crew had killed two men on the speedboat, the other two surrendered. In the boat, boxes of dollar notes and other currencies, as well as bank statements and bank transfers have been found. I said, "But there is no one who can be happy about it".

We packed our gear, thanked the SWAT Team and the Coast Guard, and headed for the boat we came with and rode back to the Coast Guard Station on Fort Myers Beach. On the way back, Snake wanted to know if we wanted to accompany him next week, he would like to visit

Chief Sam (Jumper) Obiaka again. Bert and I, declined with thanks, once is enough, we still have a sunburn on our noses, "Let's go tonight to Grimaldi's pizzeria in the Bell Tower Shops and celebrate the good guys triumphing again!"

THE END

Thanks to my friends and family who, as always, supported and encouraged me to translate this Book** from German into English. It was a hard piece of work. Special thanks to Kathryn Kick, a longtime friend of our family. Kathy is a librarian at a school in Chicago Illinois. Without her editing and proofreading of my 'amateur like' translation, this book would never been published!

Thank's, Kathy!

**Die Toten in den Everglades* Publisher BoD Verlag Germany ISBN # 9 783751 953498